Digging Deeper Into HIStory

A Study Guide for Shepherd,
Potter, Spy—and the Star Namer

Peggy Miracle Consolver

Carpenter's Son Publishing

Digging Deeper into HIStory
© 2016 by Peggy Consolver

Published by Carpenter's Son Publishing, Franklin, Tennessee in association
with Larry Carpenter of Christian Book Services, LLC.

Scripture taken from the Holy Bible, New International Version,® NIV.®Copyright © 1973, 1978, 1984,
by International Bible Society. Used by permission of International Bible Society.

Cover and Interior Design by Suzanne Lawing
Map by Lisa May
Printed in the United States of America

978-1-942587-67-5

Acknowledgements

Special thanks go to my friend Allison Pittman, author, teacher, mentor, and member of ACFW who gave me encouragement in my writing and valuable insights into what kinds of questions to include in this study guide.

As always, my deepest gratitude goes to my husband and best friend.

But all the glory goes to my Lord and Savior who led me on this amazing and exciting journey of digging deeper into His word.

Dear Students, Teachers, and Parents,

Thank you for reading *Shepherd, Potter, Spy—and the Star Namer*. The author hopes *digging deeper into HIStory* through this study guide will be a rewarding experience.

If you have any questions, comments, or suggestions concerning the book or the study guide, please contact me at PeggyMiracleConsolver.com.

Sincerely,

Peggy Miracle Consolver

Map of the Holy Land

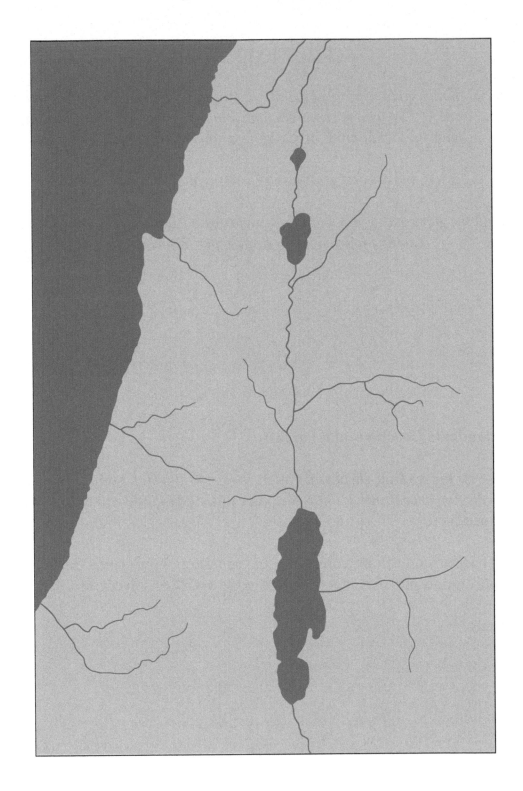

Shepherd, Potter, Spy—and the Star Namer (SPSSN)

Peggy Miracle Consolver

SPSSN is a Bible* Study disguised as a novel.

True to that concept, this companion Study Guide's main purpose is to take you back to the Scripture to read it for yourself and discover God's word is not a dusty old book of theology.

On the surface, the novel is a fictional tale of the adventures of a young boy in the Late Bronze Age. However plausible, the colorful story of Keshub and his family in Canaan in 1407 B.C. is the product of imagination. But the framework of the story from Genesis 9 to Psalm 114 is history and inspired truth.

At the same time and not so far away, a fictional nephew of Joshua experiences the events of the Hebrews' last year in the wilderness. These non-fiction events play out from Numbers 20 through the Book of Joshua. The word of God is reliable, authentic, insightful, and inspired by the Holy Spirit.

Like an archaeologist hearing the clink of his trowel uncovering pottery hidden for centuries, the reader will zero in with a soft brush to uncover hidden artifacts. Some of the buried treasures are related Bible passages. You will discover other valuable gems of insight by linking to related websites.

Get ready to dig into Joshua's story and gain a deeper understanding of the time and place of the historical setting through Keshub's tale. You will see the interconnected stories of people, places, and events in the Bible as "living and active." Their stories offer keen insights "sharper than any double-edged sword." (Hebrews 4:12)

Consult a Bible with maps or a Bible atlas to get a general idea of where events of the Bible took place. Or go to PeggyConsolver.com/ddih for a topographical map created by the author with Bible Mapper (www.biblemapper.com) that includes all locations asked for in the units of this study guide. If place names overlay each other, adjust your view setting to a closer look by clicking Control and Plus keys at the same time.

(If you are using an e-book version of this study guide, you may print the blank map provided at the author's website to use to complete the map questions in each unit of study. Post the hardcopy map to your own bulletin board, etc, for quick access.)

*Any version of the Bible will apply. Author used the New International Version.

Your first assignment: Label the major landmarks included on the Bible map on p. 4:

a) The Salt Sea or Dead Sea,

b) the Sea of Galilee,

c) the Great Sea or the Mediterranean Sea, d) the Jordan River.

Place map directions on the map on p. 4. "North" at top, "East" on right, "South" at bottom, "West" on left. (Hint: Write small with a pencil.)

As you learn more about the Gibeonites of Joshua 9 and 10, you will identify other points of interest. Knowing the geography of the setting will help you visualize the story as it unfolds.

In each unit of study you will be directed 1) to read related scriptures and write the main thought, 2) to add points of interest to your map, 3) to compare then and now in 3-5 sentences, 4) to learn more through research* and report at least one new fact, and 5) to tell how you feel about some part of the story in 2-3 sentences.

*NOTE TO PARENTS, TEACHERS, and STUDENTS:

If you have purchased the hard copy of the Digging Deeper study guide, you can access the List of Internet Links at PeggyConsolver.com/ddih to avoid having to type in links. For electronic copies, just click on the hyperlink provided within the unit. In both cases, look for the Unit number and the Question number on the List of Internet Links to find the one you are seeking. Click on the link provided to discover new insights.

Due to the somewhat fluid nature of the internet, the author cannot guarantee the links provided for further study will remain active. When a link proves to be inactive, please notify the author through the Contact function on the website. Author will make periodic updates for links in this study guide and/or at your request. Another option: with parent's permission and guidance student can use an internet search engine to find more information on the topic.

Prologue-Chapter 5   # Unit 1   pp. 15-48

Prologue: **Read** about the Gezer Calendar at the website designated at PeggyConsolver.com/ddih. Author edited the calendar to start at the season/month that correlates with the story. **Optional project:** On construction paper, devise a similar calendar that incorporates the major events of your family's year with the seasons. (Hint: Start in April.)

1. The bear encountered by a young shepherd in Canaan would be the Syrian Brown Bear.
   Examine this website: *Bears of the World,* by going to the designated website at PeggyConsolver.com/ddih
   Report something unique about the Syrian Brown Bear.

2. **Tell** how you have helped a cousin or close friend who needed your help.
   Describe how it made you feel.

3. The Late Bronze Age is a period of time over three thousand (3,000) years ago. **Compare** the lifestyle of that day with yours. How do you or your parents get news of what is happening around you? **Analyze** why it was important for the men of the village of Gibeon to hear what the caravanner had to say.

4. **Read** Numbers 20:1-13. **Report** why God tells Moses he will not go into Canaan.

5. In your Bible or a Bible atlas of your choice, **locate** Kadesh-barnea where the caravanner saw the glow of the Hebrew camp on the horizon. **Locate** Gibeon, Keshub's home. Add both to the map on p. 4.

For further study:

Abraham's son	Genesis 21.
God's promise to Abraham	Genesis 12:2-3.
Hebrews need nothing from outsiders	Exodus 16 and Joshua 5:12, also Deuteronomy 29:5.
Kadesh Barnea	Numbers 20:1.

Unit 2

1. Before books, libraries, and the internet made information readily available to all, groups of stars were visual aids for word-of-mouth storytelling. **Read** Psalm 19. **Describe** how the writer of the psalm felt when he looked at the stars. With your family, take a look at the night sky, preferably away from urban lighting. How do you feel when you gaze at the stars?

2. **Research** to learn more about the constellations in the night sky in *SPSSN* chapter 7. In modern times they are referred to as the Southern Cross and the star Alpha Centauri. Learn more at the website designated at PeggyConsolver.com/ddih. To the naked eye, Alpha Centauri is one star. **Report** what high-powered telescopes have revealed to modern astronomers about this star.

3. **Consult** a Bible reference book, such as an almanac, with a list of animals mentioned in scripture. Or access this website through PeggyConsolver.com/ddih.
How do you feel about Keshub's struggle to protect his flock? **Why** did Keshub regret his actions?

4. **Compare and contrast** Keshub's daily activities with your own. What is similar and what is different?

5. **Locate** Jerusalem, bin-Zedek's home, and Hebron, the location of the giants bin-Zedek told about (Joshua 11:21-22). Add to your map on page 4.

For further study:

Amalekites	Numbers 14:45; Deuteronomy 1:44.
Anak	Numbers 13:28-33 and Joshua 14:15.
Bear constellation	Job 9:9.
Edom, Edomites	Numbers 20:14-21.
King's Highway	Numbers 21:22.
Lion in Canaan/Israel	I Samuel 17:34.
Sons of Anak	Numbers 13:22, 28, 33; Joshua 15:13-14, 21:11; and Judges 1:10, 20.

Unit 3

1. Have you ever competed in an individual competition? Before an audience? **How** did you feel and how did you handle either winning or losing? **Why**?

2. **Compare and contrast** the differences revealed by bin-Zedek about his father in *SPSSN* chapters 6 and 12. What does this reveal about bin-Zedek? Why did the king's son ask to be called "plain Zed"? (The prefix "bin" means "son of.")

3. Using a Bible reference book on customs or a Bible almanac, **read** about the custom of arranged marriages, betrothal, and the wedding. See Genesis 24, 29. If you have attended a **wedding, describe** your experience. What are some of the differences in our customs related to marriage to what you read in the Bible?

4. **Read** Numbers 21:4-9. Compare the New Testament reference to this same event in John 3:13-21, and 19:16-19. **Report** who was speaking in the passage in the Book of John. Who was he saying would be lifted up? And what would be the result in v. 19:15?

5. **Locate** Arad, the first city defeated and destroyed by the Hebrews, and Mt. Hor in the south near the boundary of Edom. Also locate Bethel and Ai near Gibeon where the runner in chapter 13 was going next. Add them to your map on p. 4.

6. **Optional project: Research** how to make a 7-cord braid through the website designated at PeggyConsolver.com/ddih. Three, five and six strands are simpler. Choose one, and with materials available to you, such as cord, ribbon, yarn, etc., braid a seven-inch length and make a bracelet.

For further study:

Arad, Atharim	Numbers 21:1-3.
Layout of Camp of Hebrews	Numbers 2:1-34.
Naphtalites position in column of Hebrew tribes	Numbers 2:29.
Tent of Meeting, position in the camp	Numbers 2:1-2.
Elishama, Ephraimite clan	Numbers 1:10.
God's provision in Hebrew camp	Deuteronomy 8:4.
Manna	Exodus 16:4-5, 27-30.
Curse, thirty-eight years	Deuteronomy 2:14.
High priest's death	Numbers 33:37-39
Mt. Hor	Numbers 20:29

Chapters 16-20   # Unit 4   pp. 113-152

1. On your map on p. 4, **locate and label** the Arnon River flowing into the Dead Sea from the east and the Jabbok River east of the Jordan River about midway from the Sea of Galilee. According to Numbers 21:21-31, these rivers are boundary lines for the Moabites and Ammonites. Also **locate and label** Beersheba, a town in the south and Sidon, a town in the north.

2. **Check out** what is happening on Mt. Moriah in each of these references: Genesis 22:2, II Chronicles 3:1. **Describe** each in one sentence. (The two events are separated by at least one thousand years.)

3. See modern day pictures of Jerusalem through two designated websites at PeggyConsolver.com/ddih. Or search an internet search engine for "aerial view of Jerusalem." All the structures seen there are more modern than the Late Bronze Age era of Joshua. It is undisputed that the most prominent feature of Jerusalem in the present day is the same as the site of the event of Genesis 22:2. What is the name of the most prominent landmark?

4. **What** did Keshub learn about his father from watching his father's interactions with the king of Jerusalem and with Ra-gar' of Gibeon? **Describe** how Keshub's attitude changed toward his father.

5. Jerusalem's market day (on Mt. Moriah) was the closest significant buying and selling place for Gibeon (about 9 miles away). **Compare and contrast** a typical 21st century shopping trip with Keshub's experience.

For further study:

Moses and the Amorites	Numbers 21:21-23.
Manna	Exodus Chapter 16 and Joshua 5:12.
Ammonites	Deuteronomy 2:9, also Genesis 19:30-36.
Moabites	Deuteronomy 2:9, also Genesis 19:30-36.
Hinnom Valley	II Kings 23:10 and II Chronicles 28:3.
	Also Genesis 15:16.

Chapters 21-23 # Unit 5 pp. 153-177

1. In chapter 21, Keshub chatters through the whole sword practice with Da-gan'. What new information has Keshub recently learned about the bully? **Analyze how** Keshub's attitude has changed toward Da-gan'. **Why** do you think Keshub is trying a new strategy to deal with his enemy?

2. Micah mentions that honey is reserved for medicinal uses at his house. **Learn** that honey may again become an important weapon against infection in modern medicine at the website designated at PeggyConsolver.com/ddih. Read the first four lines of this professional paper to find how modern doctors describe the advantages of using honey in wound care. Also read the first paragraph of the introduction. **Why** does this new understanding of honey matter?

3. Have you attempted lashing? Many tools and household furnishings or items of camping gear can be made with sturdy sticks and rope or shoelaces and pencils! **Watch and learn** at two websites designated at PeggyConsolver.com/ddih.
Do a simple lashing project, perhaps a tripod to hold a pottery candy dish.

4. Read Exodus 16:11-36 for the provision of manna in the wilderness, and read any footnotes related to manna there. See also Numbers 21:5. **Why** do you think the Hebrews struggled with gratefulness? **Describe** how you would feel if you ate the same thing every day for forty years. What was the alternative for the Hebrews? Who does the food gathering and food preparation in your home?

5. Moses wrote of the battle with Sihon of Heshbon and Og of Bashan in two passages. Read Numbers 21:21-35 and Deuteronomy 2:24-3:11. **Locate and label** Heshbon and Jazer (Numbers 21:32) on the east side of the Jordan River on your map on p. 4.

For further study:

Refugees	Numbers 21:32
Destroy everything	Numbers 21:23-26
Child sacrifice	Genesis 15:16; II Chronicle 28:3
Moab	Deuteronomy 2:9

Unit 6

1. **Read** carefully these passages related to Balak, king of Moab, and Balaam, the seer: Numbers 22-24, and also 31:1-8. **Why** do you think God allowed Balaam to follow his own stubborn heart? Did God actually change his mind? Compare Hebrews 13:8. **Explain** in two to three sentences.

2. The NIV Bible says Balak met his returning princes and Balaam on the Arnon River "at the edge" of his territory. A dramatic edge exists on that border. **Describe** *in first person,* as if you were there, the excitement of the YouTube video taken on the Arnon River in the Arnon Gorge in Jordan in 2010. Access at PeggyConsolver.com/ddih.

3. Learn more about the Senet game purchased by cousin Lehab in chapter 25 at the website designated at PeggyConsolver.com/ddih. **Compare and contrast**, in two to three sentences, your own hand-held games to this young boy's 3,000 years ago.

4. **Read** Exodus 20:1-21. Then read Numbers 25. Which of the Ten Commandments did the Hebrews disobey that caused God to send a plague against them? **Copy** the Ten Commandments in Exodus 20 and post them on your own bulletin board or other prominent place as a reminder of God's instructions for a happy life. **Explain how** the list of negative commands can be a recipe for a happy life.

5. **Locate** Jericho and Shittim. (Bible Mapper calls it Abel-shittim.) Add both to your map on p. 4.

For further study:

Numbers 2:18-24	Numbers 26:2-51
Numbers 13:1-33	Numbers 34:24
Numbers 14:1-24	Judges 1:16 and 3:13

Unit 7

1. At least three mountains are mentioned in the area near the camp of the Hebrews while they were at Shittim. **Locate** Mt. Pisgah (Numbers 23:14), Mt. Peor (25:3), and Mt. Nebo (Deuteronomy 32:49). Add all three to your map on p. 4.

2. Check out this link to the Jewish Virtual Library through PeggyConsolver.com/ddih. **Read** about the "tell" upon which the ancient city of Jericho was built. **Report** three facts about Jericho that make it one of the most unique cities in the world.

3. In the Late Bronze Age, hunting for wild game to provide food was essential, but first you might have to make a bow. **Watch** a video accessed at PeggyConsolver.com/ddih to **learn** the basics of making a bow. **Compare** our food sources in the 21st century to Keshub's. How much time do you think about where your next meal will come from? **Contrast** that with Keshub and his family. **Research** places to go in your area where you could learn more about archery. Perhaps you and your family can explore this ancient sport.

4. **Read** Deuteronomy 31:1-8. Moses charged Joshua to lead the Hebrews into Canaan. What promise from God did Moses repeat twice in vv. 3 and 6? **Copy** the promise in v. 6 in your best handwriting and post it on your personal bulletin board in a prominent place. **Explain** in two to three sentences how you can apply this promise to your own life.

5. Read again in chapter 29, p. 221 in SPSSN where Eskie overhears Moses saying good-bye to Joshua. **Which** of Moses' words likely impacted Eskie most? **Why**?

For further study:

Instructions and Construction of the Tabernacle	Exodus 25-31:11 & 38:8-40:38
Care for the Tabernacle when moving camp	Numbers 3:25-31
Ancient relationship of Abraham to Moab	Deuteronomy 2:9 and Genesis 18 & 19
City of Palms	Judges 1:16 and 3:13

Chapters 31-34　　　　　　　# Unit 8　　　　　　　pp. 235-276

1. **Compare and contrast** Keshub's own home in Gibeon and the city of Jericho. **Why** did Keshub's attitude change toward his birthplace after his first visit to Jericho? **Describe** a time when you were disappointed in a place or event after looking forward to being there for so long.

2. Since ancient times, the Jordan River has been a natural boundary. The year-round snow cover of Mt. Hermon fed the river and contributed to its seasonal flooding, reaching its highest level in the spring months. **Locate** Mt. Hermon, the source of the Jordan River and **label** with an X on your map on p.4.

3. Access pictures of Mt. Hermon through the website designated at PeggyConsolver.com/ddih. Consult a modern map. What present day country is Mt. Hermon in? What does that tell you about who has the most control over the source of water to the Sea of Galilee, the Jordan River, and the Dead Sea?

4. **Read** Psalm 114. **Report** what natural force of nature God may have used in v. 7 to cause the waters of the Red Sea and the River Jordan to part temporarily about 40 years apart.

5. **Read** Joshua 5:1 and 10-15 and Exodus 12. List the main points about choosing the lamb for the Passover. **Compare** John 1:19-34. What did John the Baptist call Jesus?

For further study:

Get ready to cross the Jordan	Joshua 1:11, 3:3
Leader of tribe of Judah, Ephraim	Numbers 34:19, 24
Joshua appoints two spies	Judges 1:13
Possible candidates for the two spies	Matthew 1:5 & Numbers 1:7 & Judges 1:13
Thirty-eight years ago, 2 survivors	Deuteronomy 2:14-15, Numbers 14:30
Layout of Hebrew camp	Numbers 2:18
Magdalyn quotes Father Abraham's words.	Genesis 18:25
Magdalyn quotes Moses.	Deuteronomy 32:3-4
How long the Hebrews camped at Shittim	Deuteronomy 1:3
When the cloud moved	Exodus 40:36-38, Numbers 9:15-23.
Moses' charge to Joshua	Deuteronomy 31:1-8
God's instruction to Joshua and his army	Deuteronomy 31:6, 23; Joshua 1:5-9
Instructions for breaking camp, particulars	Numbers 2:2, 7:2-9, 4-6, Exodus 37:1-5
The crossing	Joshua 3:15-4:24
Hebrews conquered Gilgal	Joshua 12:23, 5:11, 4:19
First Passover	Exodus 7:1-13:16
First Passover in Canaan	Joshua 5:10
Place hands on lamb	Leviticus 4:29
Passover in the month of Abib	Deuteronomy 16:1
Joshua quotes Moses' writing	Deuteronomy 26:8 & 9:6
Manna	Exodus 16:23
No more manna	Joshua 5:10-12

Unit 9

1. The thief of Gibeon was given three options for his punishment. **List** the options. **Analyze**, did the thief choose the easy way out? **Why** do you think so?

2. **Research** ancient weapons incorporating metal through the website designated at PeggyConsolver.com/ddih. Also check out a short video of how to use a slingshot. *(CAUTION: If you try this, DO NOT USE A STONE. You are responsible for damage or injury to people and property around you, so use a small foam ball or other soft missile.)* Analyze which weapons would seem to be more effective for the soldiers of Jericho? For the Hebrews? In 3-5 sentences, **compare** Bronze Age weapons with 21st century weapons.

3. Spying on the ridge above Jericho was often monotonous. **Describe** a time when you felt nothing was happening. What did you do to fill the time? What positive strategies could you devise to pass time when *nothing is happening?*

4. The flooded Jordan River did not prevent the Hebrews from crossing. **Locate** Gilgal, the new campsite of the Hebrews on the west side of the Jordan River. **Label** Gilgal on your map on p. 4 of this study guide.

5. **Read** Exodus 25:10-22. Using the description of the ark as guide, **make a drawing** of what this most important part of the tabernacle might have looked like.

For further study:

The march around Jericho	Joshua 6 & 1:12-15
The house on the wall	Joshua 2
God's purpose in hardship	Acts 17:27
Canaanite interpretations of events	Joshua 9:9-10 & 2:9-11

Unit 10

1. On your map on p. 4, **circle the two cities** the Hebrews have attacked and destroyed to this point: Jericho and Ai.

2. **Research** the basic three elements of fire and the three sizes of wood needed to build a campfire at the websites designated at PeggyConsolver.com/ddih. **Report** what you learned by writing two to three sentences. Ask your parents to plan a cookout at a nearby lake or park where outdoor fires are allowed. Practice what you learned.

3. From Joshua 7:1-12, **explain** why the Hebrews were defeated at Ai the first time. Also read James 1:13-15. In two to three sentences **report** what this tells you about temptation and sin.

4. **Describe** a time when you, like Keshub, did a job you had considered to be a grown-up's job, perhaps babysitting, or mowing the lawn, or shopping alone. **How** did it make you feel?

5. On the second try, Joshua and his army defeated Ai. Learn about Joshua's strategy by reading Joshua 8 carefully. Summarize Joshua's battle plan in 3-5 sentences OR draw a map of the battle and indicate the placement of different players and groups in the battle. Remember east on a map is always on the right, north at the top. How many of the Israelite army went out to this battle, v. 3?

For further study:

The gate of Ai	Joshua 8:11.
Hebrew casualties	Joshua 7:5
The cause of Hebrews' defeat at Ai	Joshua 7:6-15
Judgement on Achan	Joshua 7:10-26
First mention of Hivites	Genesis 9:24-26, 10:6 & 15-17

Unit 11

1. In May of 2010 the author observed an insect on the heights above the Jordan River. On that sighting, the creature was the same color as the dusty gray-brown hilltop scenic overlook. **Research** the praying mantis or mantids at the websites designated at PeggyConsolver.com/ddih. Read more about this insect at National Geographic Kids. **Report** on what you learned in at least 3-5 sentences.

2. **Read** Joshua 9:1-15 for the Biblical account of the Hebrews' encounter with the Hivites (v. 7) of Gibeon in the Jordan Valley. **Report** what the delegation from Gibeon said their elders (v. 11) told them to say to the Hebrews. Copy the words below. What attitude did their elders want the Gibeonite delegation to have toward the Hebrews? Consider II Samuel 22:28. Copy this verse here:

3. **Locate** the other cities of Aijalon Valley that were allies of Gibeon: Kiriath-Jearim, Kephirah, and Beeroth and label on your map on p. 4. (Beeroth is not found on the map on author's website because it is so close to Gibeon. The labels overlay one another on this size map. Label Beeroth just to the south of Gibeon.) When listed on maps, the locations do not always agree. Understand many locations are approximate.

4. Knowing they might be attacked soon, Keshub's father stayed busy making shoes. **Describe** how you react in a tense situation, especially if you have to wait.

5. **Read** Genesis 9:24-27. **Report**: what was Noah's curse on Canaan? (Shem's/Abram's family line is found in Genesis 11:10-26.) **Read** Genesis 10:15-17 to find Hivites listed as descendants of Canaan, son of Ham. *If* the Hivites' ancestors passed down the fear of the curse of slavery, **explain** how the Gibeonites used that fear for a positive outcome?

For further study:

See Numbers 2:2	The organization and set-up of the Hebrew camp
See Psalm 147:4	Who named the stars?
See Joshua 1:12-15	The Gadite soldiers

1. **Find out** where Rahab hid the two spies of Jericho. Joshua 2:6. Go to the website designated at PeggyConsolver.com/ddih to **learn why** Rahab probably had flax stalks on her roof. **Report** three things you learn about the *usefulness* of flax.

2. The Sabbath observance by the Hebrews set them apart from all other people groups. **Read** Exodus 20:8-11 and Deuteronomy 5:12-21. Observance of the Sabbath rocked Ishtaba the potter's world. **Analyze** why Ishtaba would be uncomfortable with taking a day of rest? **Explain** in 2-3 sentences.

3. **Project**: Keshub asked, "Can God see what is in my heart?" **Read** Genesis 6:5 and 24:45. Also Psalm 119:9-11. Copy verse 9 on unlined paper, **embellish** with colored pencil and post it on your bathroom mirror.

4. **Read & Report:** What names did Moses use for God in Deuteronomy 32:1-12 and v. 40? List them below. **List** the descriptive words Moses used to proclaim and praise the greatness of their God in vv. 3 and 4?

5. **Locate** the other four Amorite city-states whose kings were in alliance with Adoni-Zedek, king of Jerusalem: Hebron, Jarmuth, Eglon, and Lachish. Label these cities on your map on p. 4.

For further study:

See Genesis 35:16-18	Jacob's twelve sons
Exodus 40:34-38	When to break camp and set out
See Deuteronomy 6:4-5.	The Hebrew Shema, often recited by families
See Joshua 3:1, 6:12, 15.	Joshua's habitual rising time

1.   **Locate** the pass of Beth Horon, which is at or near the site where Joshua asked God to make the sun stand still until the battle was won. **Label** this site on your map on p. 4.

2.   Dr. James B. Pritchard, an American archaeologist from the University of Pennsylvania, led four digs in the area of a Palestinian village called "el Jib" in 1950-61. He conclusively identified the location as the Biblical site of Gibeon. (Conclusive archaeological evidence is rare. There is usually room for debate.) In his book about his finds, Dr. Pritchard stated *he found no evidence of a wall around Gibeon until after the arrival of the Hebrews.* (Emphasis added.) **Read** the only description of Gibeon in the Book of Joshua in 10:1-2. a) **Report** what two ways Gibeon was stated to be "like one of the royal cities". b) According to the story, describe what ways Ishtaba and the men of Gibeon had established Gibeon as an "important city."

3.   Read again p. 367 in *SPSSN*. In 3-5 sentences, **compare and contrast** Micah's rational assessment of the threat to their survival and Keshub's hope that help would arrive in time to save them.

4. **Read** God's promise to Abram in Genesis 12:3. **Explain** how God's promise came true for the Hivites of Gibeon and their neighbors.

5. **Read** Genesis 50:20 which Joseph said to his brothers who sold him into slavery. **Explain** how Joseph's words apply to the Gibeonites?

6. **Optional**: If you are intrigued by archaeology and recent finds related to Bible history, you will enjoy exploring the website designated at PeggyConsolver.com/ddih. Report on one new discovery in 2-3 sentences.

For further study:

See Psalm 19:1-4.	God's creation speaks of his glory and power.
See Genesis 15:16,	God's grace, law, and judgment
Leviticus 18:21; 20:2-5; 20:22-24	regarding unspeakable practices.
See Joshua 3:1, 6:12, 15.	Joshua's morning routine

Answer Key

Unit 1, Prologue-Chapter 5

Prologue: Student will make a family calendar with important events added.

1.1 The only bear with white claws

1.2 Student's experience regarding helping someone else in a difficult time.

1.3 Then: no stores, no newspapers or TV or internet. Caravans were an important source of information about what was happening beyond their valley.

1.4 Moses did not enter Canaan because he struck the rock instead of speaking to it as God specifically instructed him. "You did not trust me enough to honor me as holy…."

1.5 Map work. Locate Kadesh Barnea and Gibeon, cities or villages in the story.

Unit 2, Chapters 6-10

2.1 The writer of Psalm 19 was seeing God's glory through the wonder of the night sky. Plus student's expression.

2.2 Alpha Centauri is three stars in one when seen through a high-powered telescope.

2.3 Student's feelings and interpretation. The need to protect the family's flock produced conflicted feelings because Keshub admired the beauty and strength of the animal.

2.4 Keshub carries water, tends sheep, walks everywhere; we turn on faucet, feed the dog, walk the dog, drive most every place else. Keshub spends most of his time outside doing physical activities. At 11 he is attending a military training school. Similar: both do chores, help mother, etc.

2.5 Map work. Locate cities of Jerusalem and Hebron.

Unit 3, Chapters 11-15

3.1 Student's experience on competing and winning or losing.

3.2 The first time they met, bin-Zedek was bragging about his father but probably was trying to keep up appearances. By the second time, he did not want to bear his father's name. He became plain Zed.

3.3 In the Bible parents often chose a wife for their son. Young people did not date. Today, an official of the church and/or state conducts the ceremony. Other from student's own experience.

3.4 O.T., serpent lifted on a pole in middle of camp in desert. N.T., Jesus said He must be lifted up like that serpent, and later He was lifted up on a cross outside of Jerusalem so that "everyone who believes in Him will have eternal life."

3.5 Map work. Locate Arad (a town) and Mt. Hor in the south and the towns of Bethel and Ai in the north.

3.6 Optional Student project: braid a bracelet.

Unit 4, Chapters 16-20

4.1 Map work. Locate and label the Arnon R. and the Jabbok R. on the east side of the Jordan River. Indicate approximate territory of Moabites and Ammonites. Place Beersheba in the south and Sidon in the north.

4.2 Abraham and Isaac on Mt. Moriah; Solomon builds temple of God on Mt. Moriah.

4.3 Today, the most prominent landmark of the city of Jerusalem is a square area with a building with a golden dome. It is called the Dome of the Rock.

4.4 Baba was a quiet man, but strong of character and will. Baba was not a fighter, but ready to defend his son and did not bend to Zedek's pressure or Ra-gar's criticism. Keshub gained a greater respect for his father.

4.5 We go to nearby malls and even neighborhood stores in our cars, seldom walking there. We pay cash or credit. We rarely trade goods or services.

Unit 5, Chapters 21-23

5.1 The bully has no mother and no coat or cloak. He spies on the Ra-eef' courtyard probably because he's lonely or afraid when he is alone at night when his father is night watchman. Keshub has new sympathy for the needs of Da-gan'.

5.2 Honey keeps the wound moist and covered. It prevents microbial infection. This is significant because more and more microbial infections are becoming resistant to modern antibiotics.

5.3 Student's hands-on project: Lash a small ladder, tripod, etc.

5.4 They couldn't see the God who provided manna. Perhaps their appetites were stronger than their faith. Unless there was a creative cook, the food was bland and always the same every day for forty years. Without manna they would have used up their supplies in a short time in the desert. Add student's own experience.

5.5 Map work. Label the cities of Heshbon and Jazer east of the Jordan River.

Unit 6, Chapters 24-26

6.1 Perhaps God allowed Balaam to go to Moab because of Balaam's greediness, but God used Balaam to bless the Hebrews instead of curse them. Balaam's willfulness did not go unpunished. God did not change his mind.

6.2 Student's expression of first-person account of hiking through rushing waters of the Arnon Gorge.

6.3 A hand-held game today usually involves electronics, is battery operated. Electricity was not discovered until the 1700s. Today's games are visual and action/re-action oriented. Then the game was mental and challenged the person to think strategically.

6.4 Number One: "You shall have no other gods before me." Some of the Hebrews bowed down to foreign gods—Number Two says do not bow down or worship other gods. Each negative rule has a negative consequence when disobeyed. Obedience brings peace with God and no negative consequences.

6.5 Locate the city of Jericho west of the Jordan River and Shittim on the east side.

Unit 7, Chapters 26-30

7.1 Map work. Locate three mountains near Shittim: Mt. Pisgah, Mt. Peor, and Mt. Nebo.

7.2 Jericho is perhaps the oldest city in the world. It is the lowest city in the world at 800 feet below sea level. Historically, it was at a crossroads for many ancient nations.

7.3 We don't have to hunt. Meat is readily available at a grocery store. We rarely need a weapon. Water is available everywhere you go. We don't have to carry water with us everywhere we go. Find archery ranges in area, if available.

7.4 "He will never leave you nor forsake you." Student's own experience about being strong and courageous.

7.5 Eskie heard Moses say "God will destroy these nations before you, and you will take possession of their land." This had to be frightening to hear the Hebrews' intentions so bluntly. Also, the words "He will never leave you nor forsake you" had to cause wonder in Eskie's mind. He had only known about the local gods his father scoffed at as no gods at all. He had to wonder what it would mean for this God to go with them and fight their battles for them.

Unit 8, Chapters 31-34

8.1 Jericho was crowded and closed inside a tall wall. Gibeon was in a green valley and open to fresh air and sunshine. Keshub's attitude changed because Jericho was crowded and smelly. Student's experience follows.

8.2 Map work. Locate Mt. Hermon north of the Sea of Galilee and Lake Huleh.

8.3 Mt. Hermon is in Syria; therefore, Israel does not have control over the source of a great part of their water.

8.4 v. 7 "Tremble, O earth, at the presence of the Lord." Perhaps an earthquake caused by the presence of God held back the waters of the Red Sea and the Jordan.

8.5 The Passover lamb must be 1 year old, not ill (kept for 14 days to test this), no defect. John the Baptist said when Jesus appeared at the Jordan, "Look, the Lamb of God, who takes away the sin of the world."

Unit 9, Chapters 35-37

9.1 The options were branding and exile, military execution, or one year of confinement and forced labor. The thief chose one year of confinement. Student's opinion follows.

9.2 The swords and such were hand-to-hand weapons effective in close encounters. The Hebrews were out of range. Sling stones or other projectiles would be better, but probably still out of range. There was nothing to do but wait. Today's weapons go long distances with electronic guidance systems. War is very different now.

9.3 Student's experience of a time when "nothing was happening."

9.4 Add Gilgal to the map on p. 4.

9.5 Student's drawing interpreting the description of the ark of Exodus 25.

Unit 10, Chapters 38-40

10.1 Map work. Circle the two cities destroyed by the Hebrews on the map on p. 4.

10.2 Elements of fire: fuel, heat, air; three kinds of firewood needed: tinder, kindling, wood

10.3 The Hebrews were defeated because one of them had stolen loot from Jericho: a garment and gold and silver. God does not tempt us. We are tempted of our own desire. We are answerable for our own sin.

10.4 Student's experience in doing a grown-up's job.

10.5 Student's drawing or: Whole army went this time. Joshua divided his army. One unit hid in ravine behind Ai. Second unit camped in full sight of Ai and attacked at daybreak. Second unit of Hebrews drew Ai's soldiers out when they faked a retreat. With Ai's soldiers outside of Ai, first unit attacked city and set it afire. Second unit halted retreat and attacked. Ai's soldiers were surrounded and defeated.

Unit 11, Chapters 41-42

11.1 The praying mantis is carnivorous, sometimes eating small animals like frogs and lizards, usually eating the head first. Their heads swivel 180 degrees. They can change colors. There are over 1800 species worldwide.

11.2 In Joshua 9:11: "We are your servants, make a treaty with us." Elders advised delegation to present themselves with humility. Verse in II Samuel 22:28 says, "You save the humble, but Your eyes are on the haughty to bring them low."

11.3 Add allied cities near Gibeon: Kiriath-Jearim, Kephirah, and Beeroth.

11.4 Student's own experience about what to do when you have to wait.

11.5 Noah cursed Canaan, ancestor to Hivites, to be slaves to Shem, ancestor of the Hebrews. The Gibeonites/Hivites asked for a treaty and said (9:8), "We are your servants."

Unit 12, Chapters 43-44

12.1 Rahab hid the 2 spies on her roof under stalks of flax. The botanical name for the flax plant actually says it is highly useful: Linum usitatissimum. It has been grown and used for thousands of years. It was highly favored by the ancient Egyptians whose fine linen was traded all over the world.

12.2 Ishtaba depended on himself and his family. Each was expected to work hard every day so they would have something to eat each day. For Ishtaba to rest one day a week and recognize his livelihood came from God was a difficult change of mind.

12.3 Student project. Copy and post Psalm 119:11 on bathroom mirror.

12.4 Names of God (Deuteronomy 32:1-12, 40): Lord, The Rock, Father, Creator, the Rock your Savior. God's character is: He is great, His works are perfect, His ways are just, He is faithful, does no wrong, upright, He lives forever (v. 40).

12.5 Add the four Amorite cities that were allies of Jerusalem: Hebron, Jarmuth, Eglon, and Lachish.

Unit 13, Chapters 45-46

13.1 Map work. Add the pass of Beth-horon to the map.

13.2 Joshua 10:2, Gibeon was larger than Ai and its men were trained fighters. Other factors may have been: Gibeon was a major stop for caravans because of its reliable year round spring. And its fertile land produced grain and produce needed by others.

13.3 Micah was seeing the situation through man's eyes. They were vastly outnumbered. It was hopeless. Keshub believed Joshua would arrive in time, and with Joshua and his God on their side, Keshub had faith the Gibeonites could not lose.

13.4 The Hivites of Gibeon (Keshub's family) asked for a treaty with the Hebrews and got it. The Hebrews kept their word and fought against those who were attacking the Gibeonites. God blessed those who sought friendship with the Hebrews and destroyed those who opposed the Hebrews and their allies.

13.5 Genesis 50:20, "You intended to harm me, but God intended it for good…." Noah's curse of slavery was intended to harm Ham's descendants, but slavery saved the lives of the Hivites of Gibeon.

What did you learn?

(To the Teacher or Parent: Can the student answer ten basic questions from the Bible? Author suggests giving this evaluation orally, if possible.)

1. Name the three major bodies of water on any map of Canaan?

2. What were the two unusual things that stood over the Hebrews in the wilderness, when they traveled and when they camped, that observers could see from a distance?

3. List three activities that would be common in daily life in the Late Bronze Age.

4. In John 3, Jesus referred to an O.T. event about a serpent. What was the event, and what did Jesus compare it to?

5. What is the most well-known city of Israel in modern times as well as in the time of Jesus, and in the story of the Gibeonites?

6. Name the major river that flows from Mt. Hermon in the north to the Sea of Galilee and on south to the lowest body of water in the world, the Dead Sea. Can you relate one famous event of the Bible that happened on this river?

7. In your own words, relate three or more of the Ten Commandments. Can you find them in the Bible? Where?

8. Who was the leader of the Hebrews in their wilderness wanderings? Who did he appoint to lead the people into Canaan?

9. Draw a compass and place N, S, E, and W in their proper places. If you were in Jerusalem, what direction would you go to reach Jericho? Gibeon?

10. From this study guide and its activities, what scripture has impacted you most?

Answers to Student Evaluation:

1. Mediterranean Sea/Great Sea, Dead Sea/Salt Sea, Sea of Galilee
2. A cloud by day and a pillar of fire by night led the Hebrews or stood over them.
3. Carrying water, gathering firewood, herding sheep
4. The event: Moses raised a bronze serpent on a pole in wilderness. Jesus referred to it in predicting his own crucifixion.
5. Jerusalem
6. The Jordan River.
7. Any of ten listed in Exodus 20.
8. Wilderness: Moses. Into Canaan: Joshua.
9. Top/north, right/east, bottom/south, left/west. Jericho is NE and Gibeon is NW of Jerusalem.
10. Student's choice.

List of Internet Links

Note to Teachers, Parents or Guardians regarding internet links included in this study guide:
You may want to inspect the internet links provided in this study and listed together here for your conve-
nience. All were active as of publication. Periodic updates will appear at PeggyConsolver.com.
Please understand neither the author nor the websites proposed for further research can control all the pop-
up and side-bar advertisements that may appear at those sites.

Intro:

Go to author's website: PeggyConsolver.com/ddih to see the answer map with all sites asked for in this study guide. (Author's copyrighted map made with tools provided at BibleMapper.com.)

Unit 1:

http://www.bible.gen.nz/amos/archaeology/gezercal.htm.
http://www.bearsoftheworld.net/syrian_brown_bear.asp

Unit 2:

http://earthsky.org/brightest-stars/alpha-centauri-is-the-nearest-bright-star
http://natureisrael.com/mammals.html

Unit 3:

http://nrich.maths.org/5778

Unit 4:

https://www.google.com/search?q=An+aerial+view+of+Jerusalem&espv=2&biw=1069&bi-h=491&tbm=isch&imgil=bbz5ltRtbaEs5M%253A%253Bq9c48-MNaf4Y1M%253Bhttp%252
53A%25252F%25252Fjerusalemworldnews.com%25252F2012%25252F03%25252F29%2525
2Fthe-politics-of-jerusalem%25252F&source=iu&pf=m&fir=bbz5ltRtbaEs5M%253A%252C-q9c48-MNaf4Y1M%252C_&usg=___64VIGC_RhA-gwucssQdggbxcmM%3D&ved=0a-hUKEwjY9uyu1PLMAhXD4yYKHSrJBO0QyjcIJw&ei=2kFEV9ihKsPHmwGqkp-PoDg#imgrc=n68i4g43h6s10M%3A

http://www.sacred-destinations.com/israel/jerusalem-dome-of-the-rock

Unit 5:

http://www.ncbi.nlm.nih.gov/pmc/articles/PMC3609166/
http://www.animatedknots.com/lashtripod/#ScrollPoint
https://www.youtube.com/watch?v=Y_iGkv36dww

Unit 6:

https://www.youtube.com/watch?v=RgV2cbgJcCE
http://www.oocities.org/gabrielleblair/senet.html

Unit 7:

http://www.jewishvirtuallibrary.org/jsource/vie/Jericho.html
https://www.youtube.com/watch?v=rKABQbNuKeE

Unit 8:

https://www.google.com/search?q=mt+hermon+pictures&espv=2&biw=1366&bi-h=643&tbm=isch&imgil=9-uodU4ssE-g_M%253A%253BD5v5onFFosU-kuM%253Bhttp%25253A%25252F%25252Flooklex.com%25252Fe.o%25252Fmt_hermn.htm&source=iu&pf=m&fir=9-uodU4ssE-g_M%253A%252CD5v5onFFosU-kuM%252C_&usg=__UeLFFtaL20KURNshDeGF_Jlb9mI%3D&ved=0CDEQyj-dqFQoTCNeK49vPhsYCFUY0rAodCOEARg&ei=P_Z4VZfvN8bosAWIwoOw-BA#imgrc=1FwYPDkBWpiu-M%253A%3BAzHLpwAABwvOnM%3Bhttp%253A%252F%252Fzitnay.com%25a1%252FMt_%252BHermon%252Band%252BHula%252BValley.jpg%3Bhttp%253A%252F%252Fzitnay.com%252Fgallery%252Fv%252Fdrewandchelsea%252Fisrael%252Fchelsea%252Fday3%252FMt_%252BHermon%252Band%252BHula%252BValley.jpg.html%253Fg2_imageViewsIndex%253D1%3B3072%3B2304

Unit 9:

http://www.weapons-universe.com/Swords/Bronze_Age_Weapons.shtml
https://www.youtube.com/watch?v=lSreXRMhrO4

Unit 10:

https://smokeybear.com/en/about-wildland-fire/fire-science/elements-of-fire
https://www.rei.com/learn/expert-advice/campfire-basics.html

Unit 11:

http://www.nature-of-oz.com/mantids.htm
http://kids.nationalgeographic.com/animals/praying-mantis/#praying-mantis-eyes.jpg

Unit 12:

http://www.wildfibres.co.uk/html/linen_flax.html#History

Unit 13:

http://www.bible-history.com/archaeology/news/

Bibliography

Bernstein, Burton. *Sinai: The Great and Terrible Wilderness.* The Viking Press, New York, 1979.

Brickell, Christopher and Zuk, Judith D., editors-in-chief. *A-Z Encyclopedia of Garden Plants.* DK Publishing, New York, N. Y., 1997.

Bullinger, E. W. *The Witness of the Stars.* Kregel Publications, Grand Rapids, Michigan 49501, 1967, Reprint of 1893 edition, p. 40.

Byers, Gary. "Before They Were Sherds: Pottery Making and Use in Bible Times," Lecture, May 23, 2010, *The Search for Joshua's Ai at Khirbet el-Maqatir.* Associates for Biblical Research, Archaeological Dig, May 19-June 5, 2010.

Darom, Dr. David. *Beautiful Plants of the Bible*, Palphot Ltd., Herzlia, Israel. [No date given.]

Davidson, Robyn. "Alone Across the Outback. . ." *National Geographic,* May, 1978.

Freeman, Donna. Owner and vintner of Briar Creek Vineyards, Tyler, Texas. Quote. National Garden Clubs, Inc., Environmental Studies School I, field trip with tour of vineyard, August, 2009.

Gower, Ralph. *The New Manners and Customs of Bible Times.* Moody Press, Chicago, 1987.

Grimshaw, John PhD. *The Gardener's Atlas: The Origins, Discovery, and Cultivation of the World's Most Popular Garden Plants.* Firefly Books, Ltd., Willowdale, Ontario, 2002.

Homer. *The Odyssey of Homer,* Translated by Butcher, S.H. and Lang, A. Grolier Enterprises, Corp. Danbury, Connecticut, 1986.

Marcy, Randolph B, Captain, U.S. Army. *The Prairie Traveler.* Applewood Books, Bedford, Massachusetts, 1859.

Packer, J. I.; Tenney, Merrill C; and White, William, Jr. *The Bible Almanac: A Comprehensive Handbook of the People of the Bible and How They Lived.* Thomas Nelson Publishers, Nashville, 1980.

Park, Linda Sue. *A Single Shard.* Random House, Inc., NewYork, N.Y., 2003.

Perrins, Christopher, editor. *Firefly Encyclopedia of Birds.* Firefly Books Ltd., Abingdon, Oxfordshire, United Kingdom, 2003.

Pritchard, James B. *Gibeon: Where the Sun Stood Still.* Princeton, New Jersey: Princeton University Press, 1962.

Pritchard, James B. *The Harper Atlas of the Bible.* Harper & Row, Publishers. New York, 1987.

Rockefeller Museum, Jerusalem, Israel & Bible Lands Museum, Jerusalem, Israel: "Middle Bronze Age" Exhibits: "Bronze Hittite Sword" and "Basalt Potter's Wheel," June 2, 2010.

Schlegel, William. *Satellite Bible Atlas: Historical Geography of the Bible, 2nd Edition.* Israel, January 2016.

St. John, Robert. *Roll, Jordan Roll: The Life Story of a River and Its People.* Doubleday and Company, Inc. Garden City, N.Y., 1965.

Tubb, Jonathan N. *Peoples of the Past: Canaanites.* The British Museum Press, London, 1998.

Webster, Donovan. "Empty Quarter" *National Geographic,* Feb. 2005.

Weeks, Kent R. "Valley of the Kings" *National Geographic,* September 1998.

Wright, Paul H. Holman *QuickSource Guide: Atlas of Bible Lands.* Holman Bible Publishers, Nashville, Tennessee, 2002.

Internet Searches

Bears of the World Website. http://johnlittle.us/pfiles/jeruzoo/sldshow/animals6.htm, September 18, 2013.

Bennet, David P. *Bible Mapper: Map Development and Research Tool, Version 3.0.* 2005-2008.

Gascoigne, Bamber. "History of Counting Systems and Numerals" HistoryWorld. From 2001, ongoing. http://www.historyworld.net/about/sources.asp?gtrack=pthc

Hillel, Geva. "Jerusalem—Water Systems of Biblical Times." February 6, 2013. http://www.jewishvirtuallibrary.org/jsource/Archaeology/jerwater.html

Alpha Centauri (Toliman): http://en.wikipedia.org/wiki/Alpha_Centauri and http://en.es-static.us/upl/2009/06/Southern_Cross_Jv_Noriega_Philippines_4-29-2012.jpeg

Natural Dyes. June 21, 2014: http://www.darkrye.com/content/natural-dye-color-chart

Ancient Foods of Middle East. http://reluctantgourmet.com/vegetables/item/851-fava-beans

History of Tatoos. http://www.bodydeco.co.uk/history.htm. Bodydeco Limited, 47 Station Road, Keswick, Cumbria, CA12 4TW, August 12, 2013.

The Ostrich: http://www.ynetnews.com/articles/0,7340,L-3240850,00.html (Ynetnews.com dated 4.17.06)

Wildlife of Israel: http://en.wikipedia.org/wiki/Wildlife_of_Israel

Pritchard, Dr. James B. University of Pennsylvania: http://www.penn.museum/sites/Canaan/Collections.html *Canaan and Ancient Israel @ the University of Pennsylvania Museum of Archaeology and Anthropology.* 1999.

CPSIA information can be obtained
at www.ICGtesting.com
Printed in the USA
BVOW10s2017140916

462172BV00004B/11/P